For B & J & Norman
with affection

THE LOVE OF RICH WOMEN

Also by William Hamilton

COLLECTIONS OF CARTOONS

William Hamilton's Anti-Social Register
Terribly Nice People
Husbands, Wives and Live-togethers
Money Should Be Fun

PLAYS

Save Grand Central
Plymouth Rock Isn't Pink
Happy Landings

The Love *of* Rich Women

William Hamilton

1981

HOUGHTON MIFFLIN COMPANY BOSTON

Library of Congress Cataloging in Publication Data

Hamilton, William, date
The love of rich women.
I. Title.
PS3558.A4444L6 813′.54 81-6322
ISBN 0-395-31559-X AACR2

Printed in the United States of America

V 10 9 8 7 6 5 4 3 2 1

To Monique

"That was Don Carpenter. He just said the best thing I ever heard about writing."

"What?"

"He said it's only easy when you're doing it."

"Sounds like making love."

THE LOVE
OF
RICH WOMEN

ONE

Rowena McDonald was proud to see how well Dan Novitski looked in the Rocky Mountains. The wilderness appealed to her in its current, popular way. She never considered it ominous, as pioneers might have. Nature was the opposite now, a vulnerable place she wished to protect from even the tiny visual stings of beer cans, which could ruin the effect of an entire mountain meadow.

Dan cast. When he fished, he was as concentrated as he became on the first question of a final exam. Ro smiled. He had good bones. Her mother doted on cheekbones, the only feature on which old age could be gracefully hung. He was fabulous-looking in the wilderness.

Whoops! Like a light going on, Dan had hooked a fish. Ro jumped up, with her fists balled, and shrieked. He grinned, and the caught fish went this way and that, fluctuating the fine and delicate rod and line.

"Cimabue!" he expostulated gleefully and pulled the flapping, shiny, magic banana out of the dappled pool.

"Wow!" said Ro, loving the way Dan's favorite expostulation was the name of a thirteenth-century Italian painter. (Fra fucking angelico! was another one she liked to hear.)

Their tent and packs were of tasteful but unnatural shades of blue and orange so as not to be lost on a trek in the earthy hues. Their tent was taut with points and curves planned by Scandinavian computers to maximize volume while minimizing weight for the modern hiker. It looked like an attractive alien landed in the most beautiful possible earth site.

"I hate the way their eyes turn white," observed Ro of the grilling fish, "like aspirins."

"Should have brought some little shades from a Barbie Doll," he answered.

Cheekbones, a strange sense of humor, and a great body. Rowena was proud to be in the American wilderness with Dan.

He was from Boise, Idaho — a native of the state. She had met him at a fraternity party after the hooting and wobbling were well underway. He wasn't particularly drunk, which she thought was original. Rowena had been brought up to seek the best.

"Drink the wines of the region wherever possible," her father always advised.

"It's part of really being somewhere, drinking its wine and water — unless of course you're here." All the guests laughed as he raised a glass of great French wine to salute them at one of those elegant dinners at the house in Connecticut.

"Everyone in America drinks French water," noted the asphalt-black prime minister next to Ro's mother (who only offered a strained smile to the dinner party).

"Yes, this is from Lourdes," retorted Ro's famously witty father.

Dan was the best of the local wine available at the university, and Ro had gotten him as deftly as he'd got aspirin eyes out of the pretty pool of the mountain stream. She just focused on him at the party, and waited. She was like a ray.

"Here." He produced a spoonful of trout roe.

"Caviar," he explained.

"Gross," said Ro.

"It's great."

"That fish was a woman — gross-out!"

"OK."

When he ate it, Ro wished she had. A hot toke sent time off its line into blobs and pools in which words and food and eventually Dan came into her. Their sleeping bag wiggled like a pregnant chrysalis with the butterfly of love. Dan screamed and groaned as he shot her full. She gripped him and pumped out an orgasm of her own.

"That fish we ate was like me," said Ro as she groomed her blissfully spent lover, so attractive in the backlighting from the campfire. The tent walls leaped with spasms of shadow when the fire changed.

"I don't get it," said Dan, smiling, his eyes closed.

"Knocked up," said Ro.

Dan opened his eyes.

"What?"

"Yes."

"Are you serious?"

"I've been checked out."

Dan levered up, wide-eyed, and looked at La Madonna. The light, he noted, was straight out of the seventeenth-century French painter Georges de la Tour.

"Ro, are you?"

"Yes."

"Baby." He embraced her. She was rather beautiful in the light. Her frizzed hair was golden smoke. Her roundness, the look on her face, pregnant!

Holy shit, he thought. When the fuck did that happen? But he said, "That's beautiful."

"It's OK," said Ro, resignedly. "I'll get it fixed."

The soft golden bliss was washed away in a shocking cold splash. The connection between fornication and reproduction changed from a biological abstraction to actual circumstance, a coup at the palace, a whole new ball game.

"Abortion?" asked Dan. The fire roared with laughter at the comedy in the tent. Dan felt like a man on Main Street with no pants.

"No sweat."

"Wait a minute."

"I feel great."

"Take it easy, Ro."

"Hey, let's worry about it in the morning. I'm so stoned and sleepy and I love you," she said and she fell asleep in his arms.

Dan lay in a tent with a pregnant Eastern girl in his arms. A rich one, rumor had it. The new regime of circumstance issued thousands of directives. His affiliation with her had suddenly intensified, like a slide coming into focus from a bunch of happy, goofy dots of color.

He'd never even been east. East was museum names to Dan from History of Art. The Metropolitan Museum of Art, the Fogg, the National Gallery, Corcoran, Wadsworth Atheneum, the this and the that collection, the Boston Museum of Fine Arts, Albright-Knox — names like the stickers on the trunks and suitcases of old-time travelers, the grand luxe hotels where the wealthiest art stayed — pictures he studied only as slides. Their residence was part of their identification: title, painter, date, and location. *Rowena Pregnant* by Dan Novitski on loan to a tent in the Rockies from an Eastern collection.

Dan wanted to get out of the bag and take a walk, to breathe in the high night, but he didn't want to disturb La Madonna. Was he inside her now? A homunculus of Dan Novitski, a little dot of his own genetic memory, Jonah in the whale?

Rowena's proximity elated Dan. He held his lovely biological bride. At least for tonight they were the ancient trinity of mother, father, and child. He was thrilled. Her frizzy hair tickled him. When he couldn't stand it another second, he eased away from her. Why as soon as he admired being locked in an embrace with her did its discomforts become apparent?

That night changed the disadvantage of their hike from Ro to Dan. It had been he, easy in his mountains, calming and advising her, the outsider, making her comfortable in that incomparable ecological glamour of the Rockies. Now she was a pregnant smile and he was the outsider. She loved this power change.

"Let's worry about it when we get back," she said.

"Right."

"Hey."

"What?"

"Give me a kiss."

"Feel better?"

"I'm fine."

"So am I!"

Fishing had always been for Dan what horse-racing had apparently been for his father, an experience taking place like a bubble in the rest, in it but not of it; perfect, dry, outside, even though it floated inside that difficult substance of time and experience. Dan's father had gone off following his bubbles when Dan was five, so Dan hadn't seen much of him. Dan just fished when he could. Dan was born ambitious — too ambitious to follow bubbles.

For the first time in his life he was self-conscious fishing. He fished for Ro's eyes instead of the trout's, and it showed in his work.

"Hey, where's your luck today?" asked Ro. Dan's heart was a banging forge.

"You try it." He showed her how, held her arms like handlebars, steered her to success.

"You've got it now, I think. I put it all in you."

"Oh, darling," she said. Dan was astonished by this adult title. Darling. His mother called him darling. He had grown up as the man of the house. She smoked, sold real estate, had affairs, and loved him. She had majored in History of Art and married a man who wasn't yet a horseplayer for the same reason Ro was now ahead of him in his own country. Knocked up. Now Dan was a cause where he had been an effect.

Ro blossomed in direct proportion to Dan's worry. She laughed as much that day as she had the entire semester, a laughter pretty as wind chimes. Dan was falling in love, or, anyway, the hairs on his arms, among other things, stood up when she laughed. They'd gone together four months. He thought of her as slightly serious, a little bossy, attractive, and convenient. Now, suddenly, she had great legs, beautifully shaped, a dent of calf muscle — he didn't blame her socks for drinking her ankles into her boots.

"You keep doing that," she chided.

"What?"

She exaggerated a sigh.

"I do?"

"Like a scared cat — you know how they do that noise, hah!?"

"I'm sorry."

"No, I like it. I think it's nice. Are you scared of me being pregnant — is that why you make that cat hiss?"

"No, Christ no!"

"I'm just kidding." She commanded softly, "Another kiss."

Down they went. Great thing about meadows, always ready for it. Dan slipped his fingers in the curls that had ensnared him. He peeled it open and licked her pearl while she pulled at him with her mouth over the hill in the other valley. When inserted, he thought, This is how it happened; now it doesn't matter. Pregnancy is the ultimate birth control.

"I think I love you, Dan," she said as they watched clouds and bubbles in the coating over their eyeballs slide against the pure blue. Dan felt a great organ blast of gorgeous music and embraced her.

"God I love you too!" he shouted. "Cimabue!"

As he drove back to school, she was asleep against him. His arm about her and proud smile were symbols of the primordial protector. She wasn't really asleep. She was enjoying everything so much, watching this independent rock soften into her power, the best-looking boy in the whole school. And she loved the tingle of mountain tan on her skin. Her face and legs looked simply great.

TWO

"The Arnolfinis were what are now popularly known as the beautiful people," said the arch, popular lecturer Mr. Lewis. He struck the screen with his pointer, producing the slightly abrasive-sounding whack that he beat through his courses on European Painting.

"Young, wealthy, fashionable, and sound creatures of society buying the best of everything, in this case the services of Jan van Eyck to paint their wedding portrait.

"Giovanni Arnolfini, the groom, holds his bride's right hand with his left, signifying this is a morganatic marriage, an enviable institution we have lost — like so many other better things — in which a man of high station married a woman of lower station, with the understanding that she cannot expect either his rank or his property to be conferred upon her."

Sniggering and whispers among the students as Mr. Lewis turned like a bullfighter to address the gorgeous slide projection from another angle. "(Whack) Arnolfini's slippers, exactly the clogs whose return to fashion we hear clanking about the hallways of this university, are here, off his feet, because slippers off symbolized domesticity. Isn't this a cunning dog? It symbolizes fidelity. (Whack) Here is what charms the picture: a convex mirror showing the backs of the beautiful Arnolfinis and (whack) the front of van Eyck himself, even as he paints them.

"This is a snapshot, you see, an attempt to convey the feeling of a moment of time before the invention of the camera, a permanent kind of moment photography has stolen from us forever — the moment of the Annunciation, the moment before a drop of dew falls from the peach of a still life, a moment not of action, but of permanence, of eternity. Van Eyck has taken pains to show us this is the moment in which the Arnolfinis had their portrait painted."

Down came the pointer. In the pause, Mr. Lewis smiled widely, drawing up his audience's attention like the light change that lures trout to the surface in the evening.

"A morganatic marriage, a very specific moment, each object delineated with almost superhuman clarity, and best of all — look at her (whack), look at the bride! She's pregnant!"

The whole class broke up, snorting and snickering. How glad Dan was this was a slide show, that the lights were out, because he felt the blood of a blush as bright as a traffic light surge on.

Was the joke that old? Fifteenth century? Dan's ear lobe still glowed as the students left the lecture hall. What were they supposed to do? Get married? How did babies ever learn to talk? It was all awesome compared with the now comfortable-seeming old problems of Dan's life: unwritten papers, how to go fishing and write a paper at the same time, how to make a woman fall in love so that he could make up his mind whether or not he would reciprocate. A baby, marriage?

Because Dan was now of the same biological circumstance as that which sponsored the Arnolfini marriage, and Ro was rumored to be from the same material circumstance Mr. Lewis assigned Giovanni Arnolfini, the picture dogged him like a snatch of music. Ro didn't bulge out like that bride in the painting, but of course the blessed event was probably, how big? Two weeks — big as a salmon egg? An apricot pit? Dan was so preoccupied, his friend Alex had to slug him on the shoulder to get his attention.

"Where are you going, man?"

"Hi, Alex. Passalaqua's."

"That's what I thought. I was going to let you go and sit there until you realized you fucked up, but I had mercy when I though about what a basket case you are. There's no class, remember?"

"Oh, that's right."

"What's got into you, man?"

"It's what I got into somebody else."

"Like Ro McDonald?"

"Right."

Alex roared with a laughter so merciless, it was as loud when he inhaled as when he exhaled, a sibilant clucking checkered among loud barks.

"You going to have (pause for disgusting merriment), you going to have (once again), you going to have Jan van Eyck paint the wedding picture (again)?" The son of a bitch was in the same History of Art class. Dan gave him a body check into a tree, but Alex only kept laughing. Dan was laughing by this time, too.

*

"Doris, is my father there?" asked Ro on her telephone. She was slumped in a chair until she heard it was Doris Laitch, her father's secretary, answering. When Ro heard Doris, she straightened up and dilated her nostrils. Ro slipped into an attitude of command when she addressed Doris.

"No, dear, he's coming tomorrow."

"Oh. Can I reach him?"

"He's in an airplane, dear."

"Would you tell him to call me as soon as he's in?"

"Is there anything I can do?"

"Just have him call me. I'm coming out with a friend. We're going to drive. For the summer."

"All right, dear. Is everything all right?"

"Fine thank you, Doris."

Ro was always annoyed by Doris, a spreading middle-aged blonde who had been John Russell McDonald's secretary for twenty-seven years. Doris was plain, faithful, and hopelessly enamored of her employer.

Ro tensed her shoulders for an even less pleasant telephone call.

"Hello."

"Ro?"

"I'm coming with a friend to Connecticut second week in June. We're driving in a van."

"Where are you, Ro?"

"At college, remember? University of Colorado. Out west."

"I know that."

"The friend is a man."

"Is he black, Ro?"

"What?"

"Just kidding."

"He's a classmate of mine. He's my boyfriend."

"Good, darling."

"That's all."

"See you this summer."

Ro couldn't bring herself to tell her mother about the biological aspect of her relationship with Dan Novitski. She wanted to talk to her father about it. She wanted to annoy her father with it. It would be much more effective to tell him in the flesh, so Ro was just as glad the great man was unavailable. Just arrive and see what happened to everybody. Ro would present everyone with a new and testing circumstance: the family with pregnancy and marriage, Dan with who she was.

Being John Russell McDonald's only daughter could be wonderful if you wanted a plane to wait or felt like deflating some egotistical boy, but it was also an enormous drag: Were they kissing my breasts from lust or trying to suck out Daddy's millions? Going west and not letting on had been an act of splendid self-discipline. Ro's father admired self-discipline. He was a great sailor as well as a statesman, a financier, and an art collector. Staying unknown for four years at Colorado was the kind of thing she would reveal to him one day for his admiration. She thought it wasn't unlike casually revealing a single-handed sail around the world.

Dan's seed was planted in an Eastern treasury, and he didn't know. She had been taken for herself. Daddy would hit the ceiling!

Ro found "speed" was an enormous help in packing.

With speed, she couldn't pack enough; box after box was neatly glutted with books, papers, clothes, and memorabilia. Ebullient, happy to be doing a mundane and repetitive task, delighted to see Dan tilling the field with her, Ro had no doubt their lives as man and wife would be a splendid surprise to the Eastern establishment: a loft in SoHo, a place on the beach, baby in togs as cute as a fishing fly.

"Isn't it great, darling?" she said.

"We got B.A.'s, Ro," Dan replied, holding the documents aloft.

"And a B-A-B-Y," she replied.

Kisses and laughter: life was a matter of not making dreary mistakes. Dan was funny and handsome. Ro's pleasure tightened over the way the last book she packed filled the last interstice perfectly.

In old movies, laborious time is often passed by a fluttering calendar that stops to reveal great factories where Gary Cooper started his little mill. The van got packed the same way. They were showered, in clean clothes, too speeded up not to start driving that very night.

Driving out of the college she'd attended four years before graduation was Ro's final triumph of self-discipline. She'd done it her way. No ceremony, no parents — she left like a thief in the night, knocked up, with Dan in his van. It was romantic as bandits in moonlight.

Dan was so independent. He was the only boy in the school who could care less about the hoopla of graduation, who could leave early with her. The rest of the school were just kids compared to them. They were a couple, united by pregnancy and, soon, matrimony.

They sang and roared out onto the highway; then just drove, bright-eyed and jittery from speed, grinning like skeletons for two hundred miles. A joint helped bring the couple down in a motel still in Colorado. A van full of college past looked at them through their window as Ro closed the shade that night. The graduates didn't sleep all that well.

The plains and physiological bill for being high the day before made the next day grim. Silent and depressed, nervous and snappish, both Dan and Ro weren't all that sure their forthcoming marriage was a great idea. Driving the plains is more a passage of time than space, because of the flat sameness. Dan had never been east. Except for the gorgeous cold kiss of a morning beer, he was disappointed in the world he found beyond the Rockies.

"The only way you can tell you're traveling, is the species of run-over animal changes," he said as they passed a bashed jack rabbit, shrouded in vultures.

"Don't be depressing."

Silence and miles. Dan wondered how the pioneers ever got across it all. If it was boring at sixty, what could it have been like at four miles an hour?

"We're pioneers, Ro."

"What?"

"Heading to a new life."

"You're going to look for gold in the East."

"I've found it," he said, without, Ro hoped, knowing he had. It wasn't said sincerely enough. Their love didn't look as realistic in the day as it had at night.

"You OK?" asked Dan.

"Sure. A little sick is all."

Pregnancy provided a diversion for doubts. It made her different.

"Driving across the country may not have been so smart in this condition," said Ro. "No, I'll be all right. Forget it — it's just morning sickness."

Ro didn't want to stop. She didn't want to fly east, either. She wanted Dan to have his van in case, well, so that he wouldn't be completely dependent on her. So she could get rid of him, maybe. No, just so he could be independent. Pregnancy was depressing in the morning. You only think about the worst, when you're depressed; it's hard to believe you'll ever be happy again. When you're ill, you can only be nostalgic about being well. But then again, like the night before, when you're up, there is no down.

"Caverns!" said Dan enthusiastically, as a sign promised strange and wonderful sights in ten miles.

"Forget it," said Ro.

"Have you ever seen caverns?"

"Carlsbad and Lascaux."

"What?"

"I've seen caverns."

"You mean Lascaux, those cave paintings in France?"

"Right."

"But you can't even get into those, I thought. Because the light was fading them. Only scholars or something."

"That's right."

"How did you get in?"

"My father."

"What do you mean?"

Dan saw Ro put on her mask, as she always did when the subject of her family came up. First she put on the mustache, her index finger under her nose, then she cupped her chin with the rest of her fingers, the beard.

She scowled. Dan usually stopped the interrogation when she did this, but now he was the groom-to-be. She was always so weird about it. Who was her father? Was he a gangster? A movie star? Horrendously deformed?

"Ro, why would they let your father in?"

"They let some people in. Daddy did something for France."

It was the first time Dan heard Ro call him "Daddy." Dan was a fisherman; there was plenty of time. He decided to get the rest out whole and live, the fly fisherman's way. He pushed no further.

A pause was interrupted by another sign revealing that the cavern was five miles closer.

"Let's stop!" said Dan.

"Let's not. Those are zero caverns."

"I've never seen one."

"You'll live."

She was determined not to stop. The jilted caverns pretended not to notice as the van flew by.

Ro awoke in a gas station. She looked at the mileage. She got out and stretched and walked around to where Dan was filling the tank.

"What's wrong? It's only a hundred miles."

"Cheap gas," explained Dan.

"Look, let's just get going. I have a credit card; I'll buy the gas."

"No, that's OK."

"I mean it."

Ro got into the driver's seat. Dan looked sidelong at her. She was sure changing fast — bossy, scowling — but her leg looked wonderful, toeing the accelerator as if she were trying on the world's best high-heeled shoe. He kneaded her thigh. She was unaffected.

"We ought to start looking for somewhere to sleep while it's still light."

"You mean out?"

"Right. One of these rivers or something."

"Forget it. We're going straight through. We'll get a motel."

"No we're not."

The couple-to-be glared at each other.

"We're not, Ro. I have to save some money."

"I have a credit card. It's not going to cost you anything."

"Look, Ro, I am not a goddamn bungalow!"

"What?"

"You know."

Ro squealed with laughter. "It's gigolo, you idiot."

Ro kissed him. All the acrid tension splatted on the highway behind them. They were having a great time again.

"Look, Ro."

A sign proposed that they have a look at the largest meteor crater in the continental United States.

Ro thought it over: a meteor crater couldn't be anything but a big hole. Caverns took time; a hole couldn't take more than a minute.

"The biggest meteor ever to fall."

"All right," she said tersely. And her pretty leg striated with muscle as she hit the brake. They drove silently to the building marking the arrival of commerce to the meteor hole.

Tourists milled at the trinket counter like medieval pilgrims buying indulgences. The meteor hole was, as Rowena hoped, only a big hole explained by a periodic recorded chant describing size and scientific surmise.

Dan looked through the heavy, clumsy mounted binoculars that occluded with a clank when his quarter's worth of viewing time passed. Ro could see, without optical aid, that the other side of the hole was much like the one where they stood. The hole itself, like God, was not as understandable as the decals and T-shirts verifying the pilgrims' attendance, or the recorded authoritative description of what was known or imagined about it.

Driving back to the highway, Ro didn't have to point out she was right about tourist rip-offs.

"This trip is on me because I have to get back anyway and it's cheaper than the air ticket from Daddy I cashed in, so let's just get going. You're not a bungalow."

Dan accepted his situation. This way, he had enough to get back if he had to.

"Were your parents pissed not to come to graduation?" asked Dan.

"It would have been a big effort. Now I don't have to appreciate their big effort. I'm glad."

"You know, you're not the most sentimental person in the world, Ro."

"Thank you."

"My mom wanted to see it."

"Well, what do you want to do, turn around and go do it?"

"No. I didn't want to do it."

"Look, Dan, you're going to be wearing a silly outfit and getting your picture taken pretty soon anyway. I don't want to wait so long I need a maternity wedding gown."

"Cimabue!" shouted Dan as they roared over an orange doormat on the highway that had been either a cat or a fox.

THREE

The driveway in Connecticut had two sets of bumps built into it to slow down high-flying delivery boys. It was lined with trees. On a green, vast lawn a gardener rode a lawn mower. Dan thought it was the town park. Ro knew where the bumps were, slowing only for them as they sped to a house that was simply enormous.

"What's this?"

"This is it. Home."

"This?"

"Yes."

"It looks like the capital of something."

Ro smiled sternly as they got out and opened the back. The driveway was covered, Dan thought at first, either in pearls or babies' teeth. It crunched expensively as they disemboweled the van of their travel-mashed belongings.

A smartly tailored woman, all beige, with beige hair and a beige suit, a woman who looked like new plywood, approached them. Dan felt like the huddled immigrants at Ellis Island.

"Ro, dear!"

"Hi, Doris. This is Dan Novitski. Dan, this is Doris Laitch, Daddy's secretary."

Ro put in the part about Doris being her father's secretary because Ro felt Doris had swung out of the house like its chatelaine. Ro felt this was her house, not Doris', and Doris seemed to feel the other way around because she'd been there forever.

"Hello, Mr. Novitski."

"How do you do, ma'am."

"Just fine. Don't you want me to have someone take all this and wash it or something, Ro? You can take a swim and change for dinner. Your father's due at seven, and your mother's coming too."

"Jane?"

"Yes. She's coming out for the night. Also there'll be the Corelli-Vasconis, and Paul Steigen's bringing your father's latest acquisition. I think it's an African piece."

The pool felt wonderful to Dan. After his dive, he just hung under water a moment, rising slowly up, a fetus in the cool blue Eastern womb. Ro swam expertly and productively up and down until he halted her progress with a submarine attack. The bottom of her bathing suit floated empty to the surface like the oil slick left by a torpedo victim. Under water, her pussy was soft. It waved like seaweed in the turquoise gloom. They came up grinning out of the water. She helped him into her, sitting across him. Ro was pleased to be doing it at the house in Connecticut. It feels a little rubbery under water, but nice. They played with the possibilities offered by the lesser gravity of the aquatic environment. A gate banged. Ro pulled the floating bottom of her bathing suit back under water. That goddamn Doris approached.

"Ro, your father's arrived, but he's tied up until dinner."

Ro had Dan hidden against the wall, still in her. When Ro saw it was Doris, she hadn't let Dan out. In fact, she'd softly pinned him against the wall and bucked him in deeper so that she could look at Doris, that old maid in camel hair, without Doris knowing Ro's legs were locked around a man, his cock in her to the hilt.

"Thank you, Doris. What time is dinner?"

"I don't imagine we'll actually get to the table before nine-thirty."

Dan's head against the edge couldn't see Doris, only cool, aloof Ro astride him, looking as if they were only kissing or something. He grinned in complicity at her.

"Thank you, Doris."

The gate banged again. They laughed at what they'd done, finishing it off with a hooting frolic.

*

It was a beautiful humid evening as they walked up from the pool. The baby-tooth driveway crunched under Dan's go-aheads. Dan had been pleased by the mischief at the pool, but he felt Ro wasn't anywhere near as loving as she had been all semester. She just hadn't been as loving ever since the drive east began. Dan figured it was either pregnancy or revealing the Eastern secret that was bugging her. He was careful about challenging her about her coolness. In his fisherman's way, he was waiting to play it out of her.

Ro was thinking about that damn Doris as they approached the house. Doris had that way of making Connecticut look as if it were hers, of making John Russell McDonald look as if he were hers, and she was just a damn secretary. Ro wished she hadn't hidden what she was doing with Dan. She wouldn't, after all, have hidden what they were doing if it had been the dog standing here, and Doris was just sort of an old house dog.

Ro had sneaked into Doris' room once for a snoop. She wanted to find what it was that made Doris feel so at home, living in a room at her employer's house. Ro did find it, Doris' secret, in the wafery stack of predictably neatly folded stockings in the top drawer of Doris' dresser: a pistol.

Ro was shocked. After that, Ro never looked at Doris without thinking of that little poisonous hunk of metal hidden in the soft and gauzy underpinnings of this lonely old maid.

Because they were wet, they went in through the kitchen and up the back stairs to Ro's room. Two canopied beds were parked there like a pair of river boats. Some old dolls and early schoolbooks froze the room in an earlier time of Ro's life. Ro's bags had been unpacked there, but Dan's were apparently in another room.

"Where do they think you're going to sleep?" said Ro, looking around the room. She went to the phone, which Dan noticed was studded with buttons.

"Where are Mr. Novitski's things? Well, bring them to my room."

Ro disappeared into the bathroom. Dan, baffled and helpless, sat down and started to read *Stuart Little.* He looked at the picture between the beds. It looked surprisingly like a Chagall: flowers, peasants, flying cows, one of those peasant parties. He got up to look closer. It was real! Dan stared at it. The door opened, and a heavy, disapproving woman, a maid, he guessed, stood with Dan's backpack and suitcase, equipment that didn't go with her uniform.

"Hi," said Dan.

"I don't know how long you'll last in here when Mr. McDonald hears about it," said the woman with an Irish accent. She put the things down and left.

Dan was less at ease than ever. Ro, his only ally, was showering. A real Chagall in a girl's bedroom? He looked around: horse-show ribbons, the expectable detritus of a girl's room, teen-age equipment, cosmetics, photographs of friends, and that genuinely important painting. Dan noticed how well everything in the room — rugs, curtains, bed canopies, pillows, slipcovers, all of it — was made and maintained. It began to dawn on him that Ro wasn't just rich. She was really rich.

Ro, succulent with shower and scent, sprang out of the bathroom naked and hopped on her bed, grinning. She spread her legs and touched herself, smiling. Dan pulled off his clothes and joined her. She pulled at him, groaned, kissed him deep. When he was in, she rode him hard, playing with herself and him, kissing him on the nipples, everywhere. She was so hot and smelled and looked so good, Dan forgot everything and went along with her. She braced her legs against the bed's canopy poles. She laughed. She threw dolls around. Dan was participating in some long-considered desecration of the nursery.

"You want to do it like this?" she asked, perching coyly over flouncy pillows and a Teddy bear, her ass a valentine.

Afterward, Dan looked in his bag for one of his two preppy shirts and his only tie. To his horror, a slime of swimming pool–green toothpaste had hemorrhaged all over the tie. Ro went to get him one from her father's room. He looked at the Lolita love nest and grinned. Great sex with Ro again! It had been a while. It made Dan think he'd been restored to her passion. The love that had been so devoted and worshipful that he hadn't had to do a thing was back.

The tie she gave him was of heavy, bottle-green silk, lined in gold, with a Paris label. Dan was really starting to enjoy things. Ro, tan and flushed from recent events, looked simply beautiful in a virginal white cotton dress ahead of Dan in the upstairs hall.

Dan stopped abruptly on the stair landing; a real big Léger regarded him. "See if you can find me," said Ro, and she ran off. Dan was still staring at the picture. He looked downstairs and saw Degas pastels going down from where he stood.

Downstairs, a Brancusi sang a solo in a round, stark vestibule. Dan's jaw was down around his ankles. De Kooning, Rothko, Pollock — some he didn't even know, all real — slides come to life; like seeing a street full of Hollywood movie stars.

An old Labrador retriever was pointed at him, cranking its tail, his tongue hanging out. Dan wondered: Did this dog know about these paintings? The dog came up to him; Dan scratched his ears. It felt like a real dog. Picassos out of the corner of his eye, that startling Brancusi — Dan patted the old Lab as if he were reassuring the beast it wasn't all a dream.

Ro was gone, hide and seek in this extraordinary thing she called home. Were things like this mortal home? Were paintings painted to decorate rich peoples' houses? That purpose had never been mentioned in History of Art. In school, pictures were placed only in the abstract study of history and civilization, never in Connecticut with hot daughters and old Labrador retrievers.

The inside of Ro's house was as intrigu
cated, and total as the country Dan fished. It
magnificent manmade flora and fauna. Eve
covered with a purposeful effort of man. It
ferent from his mom's apartment in Boise. Sh
of her favorite masterpieces, some plants, a s
vague, faint echoes of the stuff in this house

Ro had scampered off, hide and seek in
knew the way Dan knew the Rockies (she wa
figure it out for himself and see how he react
she could decide what to do about him and e

Dan heard voices in convivial evening co
looked for them. In a room stood two adu
splendidly dressed. They were speaking Italiar
were natty as insects, the women as gaudy as
Dan's sneakers cringed with embarrassment
proached. He was awfully glad Ro had given h
adequate importance. Perhaps that badge
enough to satisfy them that he hadn't crawle
under the tent of this dazzling circus.

The men made unexpected, terse, smooth l
and performed unintelligible introductions. D
everyone's hand and blushed. All he'd caught al
names was that none of them was McDonald. Ma
dreds of people lived in the place, courtiers of
Now they all spoke English in deference to Dan.
ual, impressive courtesy only made him feel mo
sive.

"We are on our own for the moment, Mr. N
said a sleek Italian beetle whose remembrance
name merely intensified Dan's awareness that h
got one of the four names now regarding him

"John and Ro are closeted in the library. I guess she gives her report card. Don't you say report card?"

Holy shit, thought Dan. She's in there telling her father she's knocked up. A door will swing open; a king with a shotgun will enter. The Europeans will scatter like quail, and Dan will face the prophet's wrath.

"So let me be your host. What would you like to drink, Mr. Novitski?"

These people were art, like the rest of the room. Dan felt like a packing crate that hadn't been removed from an elegant exhibition. He wanted to apologize for spoiling the effect and run, until he dropped, west.

"Maybe a beer?" responded Dan, with instant regret. Beer? With these meticulously accoutered and toiletted Europeans? A pre-Columbian priest, his arms raised, laughed his ass off at Dan from a bookshelf that looked like a dense pine forest of leather.

The hospitable Italian looked quizzically at a little regiment of bottles in a nook.

"Perhaps in the kitchen!" he said to Dan's growing discomfort. "Ah no, here." He found a little door opening on the white humming cave of an icebox. Dan had never imagined a can of Budweiser in this setting, but, then again, he never imagined himself there either.

The man poured a glass; no one said anything. The yellow chased the white to the top; everyone watched. Dan noticed that their drinks were pale and elegant, white wine or something. He felt as if he were holding a goddamn urine sample.

"You are at university with Rowena?" asked a lady in a voice that came through a clarinet reed.

"Yes, ma'am."

"These American universities are so wonderful," the man who'd poured Dan's beer advised the rest. "So fresh and free and open, such pretty girls!"

"Yes, sir."

"It is in the West, no?" queried the clarinet. "The university of Rowena?"

"It is the University of Colorado," corrected Dan, and they laughed.

Dan's height bothered the second man more than the hospitable one. This one was shorter, nearer Dan's contemptible sneakers, than his colleague. He eyed Dan with a sidelong, bird glance, like a hen looking up for a hawk.

"They have very unusual subjects, I believe," he interjected. "You don't study philosophy or the calculus or Latin, I believe. Is it not so you study odd things such as surf-riding and skiing?"

"History of Art, actually, sir."

"Do you read Panofsky?" continued the art dealer.

"I tried," offered Dan.

"Brilliant mind, don't you think? Look, I think you will like this." He held an indoorsman's hand toward a greenish Jesus in a prettily colored crucifixion triptych.

"Boy, that's terrific," offered Dan.

"I found this for John McDonald in the Borzemena Castle," said Steigen, more to the Italians than to Dan.

"Far out."

"Yes."

In the ensuing silence, the Italian woman suddenly laughed. Everyone turned to her. She brushed off their glances with a salute and shake of her head.

"I love this expression 'far out,' " she said.

Dan felt in his pocket for the keys to his van. He almost bolted for Idaho. The suave art dealer smiled condescendingly at Dan. There was a little red thread in his buttonhole that caught Dan's eye. At first it looked like an accident, but, like everything else in this part of the country, you could see on closer inspection that it was there on purpose.

FOUR

When Ro first came down the stairs to find the Corelli-Vasconis and Paul Steigen, she had told them Dan would be along and excused herself. Then she'd gone directly to her father's study before the lost hide-and-seek player could embarrass her by shouting "Ollie ollie oxen free" from some other room.

She found her father on the phone, straining to hear a voice far away. He greeted his daughter with pantomimed smiles and gestures to a chair.

"Oui," he boomed every so often into the phone. It was the old stance she disliked so much, her father with more important things to do. Watching a man on the phone can be a humiliating circumstance. There was her father, totally involved with someone else while he looked straight at her. John Russell McDonald gave a wink and a smile and a pat on the knee to Ro and then rocked back again, concentrated, mouth ready, oblivious of her, devoting his personality to the invisible intelligence coming over the phone.

Ro felt something between her legs. She smiled. *Go ahead and be on the phone, Daddy. I think a little bit of Dan just ran out of me.* What fun it had been to talk to

Doris with Dan in her! She looked at her father, knotted in concentration, speaking scholastic French and reacting to its effect in whatever country he was addressing. Ro looked at her father and deliberately thought about sex with Dan in her flouncy white bedroom.

It took John Russell McDonald a minute to shift his intelligence from France to Ro. He stood up and gave her a subconsciously French-presidential hug and kiss on each cheek (he had been talking to the president of France). He was delighted by her growing good looks; a little woman.

"Don't you look wonderful, Ro. What a pretty dress." *Soon,* he thought to himself, *the boys will be trying to get under it.* So tan in lacy white, like a little Mexican girl at first communion.

"How's college, darling?"

"I graduated."

"What?"

That stopped him.

"Cum laude."

"Good Lord, Ro, why didn't you tell us — when did it happen?"

"I just graduated. Left early. I drove out with my boyfriend; I wanted him to meet you before you go to France." (John Russell McDonald had just been made ambassador to France.)

"Well, when was the ceremony, dear?"

"It's tomorrow. They give you a week between, and we just drove out here instead. I didn't want to bother you with it."

"I am so sorry, Ro. How would you like to fly out tomorrow with me, with both of us? Jane's coming out tonight. My plane is in Connecticut. What do you say?"

"No, Daddy, I don't want to go back; I graduated."

"I am so embarrassed. Why didn't Doris tell me?"

"It's fine. I wanted it this way. You're too busy. I don't care about things like that, and neither does Dan. So we just drove out."

"Who?"

"Dan Novitski, my boyfriend."

"You drove out here with someone?"

"Dan Novitski, my boyfriend."

"I see."

"Daddy, I'm pregnant. We're going to get married."

John Russell McDonald fell like a broken mast into a chair. He stared at Ro. It was the first time in her life she had ever had his total attention. A little scary, that attention, like being looked at by an atom bomb.

Ro was uncertain about everything in the burn of her father's stare. She felt terribly guilty. She had hurt him. He had never before seemed to her to be vulnerable. He sat staring with black eyes under wonderful baroque, cartouche eyebrows, wounded.

Ro wanted to put on a nurse's uniform and wheel him around the cloisters in a war movie. He had been horribly wounded at the front, wounded in a very private place.

She sat next to him and held his hand, an unaccustomed and therefore awkward gesture, as it turned out.

"Where is the son of a bitch?" asked John Russell McDonald, quietly, as if he were asking a scout about the whereabouts of Rommel in the desert.

"He's here."

"He is?"

Courage flowed back into the great warrior father. He stood up and glowered. Now Ro was scared. Was he strapping on a sword and buckler?

Would he hack through the wall and chop the guests to bits in a rage, reserving Dan to strangle hideously last?

"Daddy, he's wonderful. Dan Novitski."

"How long?"

"What?" For a bizarre instant, Ro thought her father was asking the size of Dan's member.

"You know."

"Just a couple of weeks."

"Well. That's not so bad. Goddamn it, Ro. Well. Don't worry about a thing, dear. I'm so glad you came to me with this."

He gave her an awkward hug. Ro was flushed with excitement.

"Don't worry, Ro," he said, opening the library door. "We'll take care of it."

*

Ro and her father made an extremely attractive pair, entering the room where Dan struggled valiantly with the Europeans.

A flutter went through the ladies, and a sort of electric current, the pleasure of power, went through the men as the great man entered, arm around his proud and pretty daughter. McDonald looked first at Dan as he strode in, grinning and exchanging pleasantries.

All sorts of alarms and thrills went off in fatherless Dan when he saw John Russell McDonald for the first time. McDonald was a tall, handsome man who seemed more vivid than anyone else in the room, beautifully and cleverly dressed. He marched straight at Dan, smiling widely.

"Well, Dan. Hello, son. Welcome to Connecticut. Ro's told me so much about you."

"Hi, sir."

"Has everybody got a drink?" Dan thought this was, without a doubt, a man so charming that all his masterpieces immediately seemed like loyal possessions, a pack of adoring hounds, instead of showy treasures.

Ro was astonished to note Dan was taller than her father. Doris had managed to sweep in with them, as though she'd been in on the conference in the library. Ro was amazed by her father's flawless and glorious cordiality. It was hard to believe this was the man in the study, the enraged slayer.

"Where is it, Paul?" McDonald conspiratorially and amiably asked the man with the Légion d'Honneur ribbon in his lapel.

"I was so pleased," gloated Paul, much more eager and less suave than he'd been before McDonald's entrance, as he directed his client to an object, about the size of a baby, wrapped in a handsome gold cloth, "to find it. I thought of you at once. It was in Helena Rubenstein's collection."

The cloth was removed by Paul with a tailor's touch.

"My God," said John Russell McDonald with awe. Shivers ran through everyone (except Prince Corelli-Vasconi, who had seen everything). It was an African mask, somber, dignified, as mysterious as deep space. McDonald's intense brooding reverence shut everyone up. It was religious in there. You expected to hear the sort of distant coughs you hear at funerals, symphonies, and coronations.

"Is it Dan, John?" asked Doris Laitch, who knew best how to play the scene of appreciating art with the great man. Not realizing the Dan were an African tribe, Dan Novitski had gone red and started to splutter. He had a sudden, startling flash of ritual sacrifice in this luxurious tabernacle, featuring himself as the offering.

"It certainly is. One of the most beautiful Dan things I've ever seen," answered John Russell McDonald, intent on the wooden visage.

"Two hundred years old, John," ladled Paul onto the already rich scene. Dan stared at the mask.

"Real nice piece," Dan chirped. Ro was astonished at Dan's effrontery. How dare he enter into her father's scene? She was also a little impressed with his courage. He might make a neat husband, after all. It made her remember how at school he was always doing confident, surprising things, like the time he disagreed with Mr. Passalaqua about the purpose of symbolism in Edmund Spenser's *Faerie Queene*. Drilled at by Passalaqua's cunning sarcasm, he held fast until, by saying "Being a teacher doesn't make you right," he got himself thrown out of class.

"Yes," replied John Russell McDonald, as though Dan's voice were coming from a chorus.

"But it can't be two hundred years old," Dan sailed on. Everyone looked at Dan now. He pointed to the brass ear ornaments.

"These are thirty-ought-six shells. They didn't have them two hundred years ago."

Paul would have garrotted this Huckleberry Duck, who belonged in this room about as much as a jukebox, had he a piece of wire and access to the light switch. John Russell McDonald looked closer.

"Quite right, quite right."

"Added much later," parried the now murderous art dealer. This son of a bitch in sneakers, who was probably fucking the bonbon in white, the daughter, had now fucked, in a sense of the word far more important to Paul, something even more precious — a sale. Yes, he would eagerly have blown the boy to bits if the means were at hand.

"Perhaps," said John Russell McDonald coolly. Clearly, his interest in the piece was gone. Church was over. Cocktail chatter resumed.

Ro was very favorably impressed. Dan had walked right into an alien landscape and pulled out a fish. She held his arm, walking in to dinner.

A handsome woman of forty-five stood puzzling over a scrap of paper as they filed into the dining room. She held her index finger like a mustache, the way Ro did sometimes. McDonald got to her first.

"Darling, you made it. This is Dan Novitski, dear. Here with Ro."

"Hello, darling," said the woman to Ro, who kissed her dutifully. "Welcome home."

"Hi."

"I'm Jane McDonald," offered the mother with enough authority to cover Ro's failure to introduce her. "Hello, Paul."

"Prince and Princess Vasconi-Corelli," continued McDonald.

"Corelli-Vasconi," corrected the hospitable prince. "Please, I am Briano and this is Giovanna."

Prince and princess? Dan was ready for anything.

As soon as he sat down, Dan knew he'd made a mistake. The kindergarten maxim "Ladies first" turned out to apply to formal dinner parties. Dan was down too soon. Paul Steigen had glanced at Ro's consternation over her lover's premature descent with a knowing smile as he stood seating her. Dan got back to his feet, attracting even more attention, as Steigen glided into his Chippendale suavely as a moonbeam.

Dan toppled back to his dining station, wishing he had on something besides sneakers. He had noted what every man had on his feet, all black, all polished — the ones of the art dealer even had some kind of little gold barrettes on them. Dan's sneakered feet felt like a pair of toilet seats. Why hadn't he packed his loafers? Some silly oversight becomes crucial once the mission is in outer space.

He looked at Ro across the round table for a smile, but she was in rosy-cheeked, animated conversation with Steigen — an attitude Dan had almost forgotten. On the trip especially, Ro's regard of Dan had accreted a gelid layer of boredom he had been able to penetrate only with his private part. There she was, looking like presents opening themselves under a Christmas tree as the art dealer chatted away in an ironic, intimate way Dan couldn't overhear. He looked at Ro's mother, finding her right next to himself, looking straight at him.

She was almost shockingly beautiful. Her skin was soft, buttered over beautiful bones. This John Russell McDonald had absolutely everything.

"Very attractive place," said Dan at unexpectedly high volume and treble. Ro looked at her boyfriend. "Very attractive": those weren't words he even used out west. She examined him. Yes, he was obviously a social climber. Cigars with Daddy after, in the library? A position with him? Soon he would be tailored and lost, anonymous, absorbed into the legions that marched for Daddy every day.

"I've never seen stuff like this except in slides," said Dan to Jane McDonald, nodding to the great Picasso behind her. "You kind of forget it was ever real." Jane's laugh led a small, approving round of laughter from the entire table that delighted Ro. Ro saw her mother was quite taken with Dan, an observation that blew a sudden surge of devotion into her connubial sail — Dan *was* terrific. For the moment, he was shining again — casting into a mountain stream with that eerie grace that thrilled Ro. She was pleased to glance around and see everyone admiring her trophy from the West.

Everyone except Paul Steigen, who loathed how easy it seemed for the son of a bitch. Some farm boy getting lucky and not having the wit or decency to admit or understand it. The bastard looked as if he were perfectly comfortable at that table, a fabulously elegant garden of crystal and silver and porcelain; forking in cuisine he didn't understand, yapping familiarly with people superior in every measure except youth, and that fancy word for ignorance, innocence. Paul nodded at the butler and pointed to Dan's fast-emptying wine glass.

"I wrote a paper that the reason so many women are, you know, buxom in those old Dutch barroom paintings is the same reason they have barmaids like that now, and Playboy bunnies — because breasts subconsciously make men want to drink. It sells more beer."

Everything Dan said made Jane laugh. It delighted Ro to have something her mother admired. Jane's nostrils vibrated, and a wide smile was playing on her face every time Ro looked. John Russell McDonald, holding forth with the prince across the table, didn't (or didn't choose to) hear most of what Dan said.

Paul Steigen talked to Ro as if she were desirable, worldly, and fully grown, something he'd never done before. It was like the surprise of a new building in what had been a field when she'd left for college. How exhilarating and grand it was to be received like a woman by a man she'd watched for years murmuring things to women that made them laugh at what appeared to be some intimate surprise.

"Go to Paris with your father," he urged. "Then we can have an affair. I'd feel absolutely disgusting if our affair were to unfold in this innocent child of a country. I would be repressed. But in Paris, breathing that ancient, worldly air, I know I would be forgiven and free."

It was the best wine Dan had ever tasted, smooth as water but deep-tasting, like drinking a shadow. Every time his glass got low, a man in a tuxedo, circling the table with a pair of maids, refilled it. He was having a great old time. Hell, these people were just like anyone, sort of.

John Russell McDonald patted Ro's brown hand and smiled.

"I want you to come over and help me in France," he said, his fancy eyebrows rising like window shades, revealing a lovely view of Paris. Ro realized what he meant was forget about marrying Dan, forget about having a baby. His big hand on hers gave a few pats and went back to his glass. He turned to Princess Corelli-Vasconi and talked about African art.

Jane laughed at Dan, making him bolder and more extravagant in his remarks.

"My dad plays the horses. I haven't seen him since I was five. He sent me a postcard from Santa Anita once. It said, 'Happy Birthday, wish I was here.' "

Jane McDonald pitched back her head and laughed.

"What are you saying so funny?" asked the woman on the other side of Dan, the princess. At the same moment, the prince began talking to Ro's mother. They were like a criminal team, thought Dan, the woman deflecting his attention so the man could grab the jewel of Mrs. McDonald's company. He had another draft from the magic wine glass that was always full.

"Oh, just about family and horse-racing."

"Ah, you have horses."

"Who, me?"

"It's such fun."

"Yes."

"My husband will not let me buy a horse. I've been dying for years to have a racing horse, but he only buys art. He tells me not only does art appreciate, its race is already won, and you don't have to buy it hay."

Dan laughed. This woman was attractive too, tits as big as football helmets. Is there any line so mystical as that formed by big breasts shelved together by a low-cut evening gown? Not to get caught staring at them, Dan concentrated on her face. "It's the first time I ever saw most of these things."

"What is your favorite?"

"Here?" (The true answer was too idiotic to admit: Jane McDonald.) "Well, I think that Léger painting is perfect for the stairs, because his paintings are real constructed-looking, like buildings going up, so it gives you confidence on the stairs. Like the stairs are well built."

This woman did not laugh. Dan had another sip of shadow. He was sure Jane McDonald would have understood. Having a remark like that out before a woman who simply stared blankly made Dan feel desperate, especially when he considered the possibility that she might think the phrase "well built" had to do with those redoubtable breasts she presented.

"That's Picasso, I bet."

"Yes it is. Nineteen fifty-seven."

"Boy, it's a great piece."

"How do you know so much about art?"

"I major in History of Art. I mean, I did. I just graduated."

"What are you going to do?"

Dan thought of her naked, in a lascivious pose, pitched forward slightly, wagging those wonderful immense tits slowly back and forth.

"I want to see New York."

"You haven't?"

"No, ma'am."

"Well, you must visit us when you do. We are one month at the Pierre." Did she know he thought she meant by "us" those breasts? Somehow she seemed to have a sense of his interest and not to mind it. Dan was surprised. After all, she was married. When he glanced around for her husband, Dan was surprised to find Paul Steigen regarding him. In fact, Steigen was pointing at Dan's wine glass to the butler. He looked quickly away.

John Russell McDonald couldn't help considering his daughter and Novitski naked, doing it. The thought made him shudder. At least the boy looked clean, even athletic. Novitski from Idaho, impregnating her, Rowena Clark McDonald. The son of a bitch. He certainly was full of himself, talking away about anything, like a goddamn salesman. America was a great country, so great it had made room for a lot of tinhorns and cheaters, salesmen and power-boat people, tasteless nobodies the powerful had to take care of with ridiculously high wages and various other free rides. But they were, after all, the voters, the consumers, the public. John Russell McDonald was all for them, of course. He just didn't like seeing them spill over into his house, into his daughter.

All the women had mysteriously vanished. McDonald, the prince, the art dealer, and Dan were there alone. Paul Steigen poured cognac for Dan. A box of cigars came forth. The men all seemed to have expected to be alone together. The prince and Steigen were chattering cleverly. Dan, grinning with drink and flushed with the effect of women's smiles, had a cigar with the rest of them. John Russell McDonald had begun to seem to Dan like a cross between Abe Lincoln and George Washington.

The men and women separating after dinner — of course! Dan got it; he'd heard of it somewhere. It was like so much of this remarkable evening, actually being in a situation you had seen only on TV.

A tool lay in the cigars to clip the tip off. Dan did that fine. The others slipped the rings off their smokes, but Dan, thinking it was both kind of pretty and reminiscent of engagement and marriage, left his on. The combination of cigar smoke and cognac was something like Quaaludes. He listened to them get exercised over the President, being by this time only slightly surprised when McDonald said things like "I told him last week it wasn't going to work," speaking, of course, of the President of the United States. Dan expected he'd be chatting with the President pretty soon, too.

"Dan," said McDonald, suddenly coming into focus from the softening spectacle Dan had begun to make of his surroundings.

"Yes, sir?" Dan felt as if he were treading water in a pleasant reverie of sex and luxury.

"Let's go in the library, son."

"Sure," said Dan eagerly. The corner of a little table nipped at Dan like a terrier as he followed his old buddy, the great man, into a high, dark, glamorous room filled with books and papers. Dan was thrilled to have McDonald call him "son."

"Real leather," said Dan agreeably, as he settled onto a sofa.

"Yes," replied McDonald.

"Sure good cigars."

"Would you like another?"

"Great."

McDonald offered Dan another cigar from a polished wooden box. Dan felt a warm partnership as the great man lit it for him. As he reached up to pluck the cigar from his mouth, he realized the one from dinner was still going in his other hand. McDonald looked puzzled. Dan held a cigar in each hand — how stupid! To cover the gaffe, Dan raised the blazing Havanas like a pair of six-guns and said, "Bang! Bang!" McDonald didn't respond.

"What are your plans, son?"

"Well, I'd sure like to see the Big Apple," answered Dan, as he awkwardly stamped out one cigar.

"Ro's told me about the problem."

"Oh, right, right."

"What are your plans?"

"Well, my uncle has a finishing camp — I mean a fishing camp — in the Rockies, and he always said any time I wanted to guide and stuff. I guess he thinks I'm pretty good. I'll tell you one thing, I do know how to fish. I can feel them sometimes, and they know it. It's like we both know it's time to get caught."

"May I ask what the hell that has to do with my daughter?"